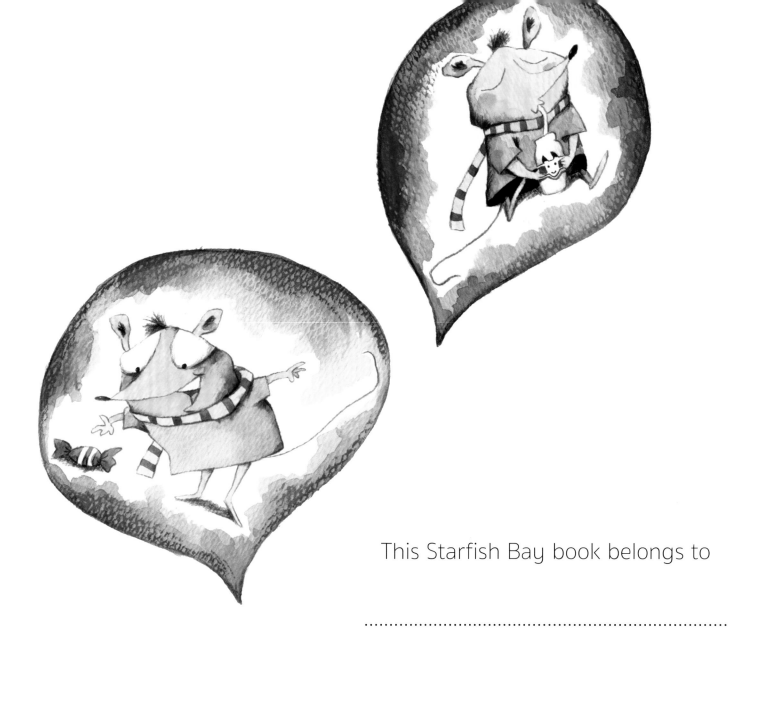

This Starfish Bay book belongs to

....

ALL SHOES COME IN TWOS

Written by Sulan TANG

Illustrated by Ke WANG

A single red shoe lay on the grass, very upset.

All shoes come in twos.
What use was a single shoe?

A little mouse saw the shoe lying on the grass. He waited by her side.

He patiently waited for the red shoe to move, so he could get the
piece of cookie beneath it.

But who knew that, from morning till night, the red shoe would not move?

The little mouse became impatient. "Are you going to leave or not?" he snapped at last. "If you don't move, I'll be very rude to you, single red shoe!"
The red shoe was a very elegant shoe.

She did not understand the meaning of "rude." "What is rude?" she asked. "Is it a style of dance? Dancing is my specialty!"

The little mouse kicked hard at a flower beside him. Petals fell like raindrops.
"Being rude is just like this. Want to see more?" asked the mouse.
The red shoe tumbled back in fright. The little mouse picked
up the cookie and strode away,
whistling quite proudly.

"I am used to being alone," said the mouse.
"And I'm now going home. Aren't you?"
"I'm lost and far from home. Without a companion at night,
I'll be afraid." The shoe was nearly in tears.

"Will you? I know little about shoes," said the little mouse. "But me? I'm always alone, outside and even at home. I'm not afraid... so long as I don't run into a cat."

By then it had grown dark, and moonlight sprinkled the grass.

"I'm not afraid of cats," said the shoe, "but I am afraid of being lonely."

The little mouse didn't know what "lonely" was. "What does lonely feel like?" he asked.

The red shoe thought for a while. "Being lonely is feeling empty in your heart."

"Feeling empty in your heart?" said the mouse. "That's impossible. Don't you mean feeling empty in your stomach? That's not being lonely. That's being hungry."

"I'm not hungry," said the red shoe.

"So, you don't eat cookies, do you?" the little mouse asked cautiously.

"Of course not." said the shoe.

The little mouse sighed with relief. "Come with me if you want," he said kindly.

The red shoe followed the little mouse across the grass to his home. But late in the night, the shoe lay awake, missing the other shoe.

"Little mouse," whispered the shoe,

"may I hug you?"

The little mouse didn't want to sleep in a shoe.

But how could he say no to the shoe's gentle request?

Without a word, the little mouse climbed into the shoe. The red shoe hugged the fluffy mouse and fell asleep.

The little mouse fell soundly
asleep, too.

The next morning, the red shoe said softly, "Little mouse, can you help me find the other red shoe?"

"I don't know..." said the little mouse. "What if we run into a cat on the way?"

"Little mouse," the red shoe begged, "please help me. Shoes always come in twos!"

The little mouse hesitated. "All right," he said finally.

And off they went. But the little mouse regretted his decision all the way. "How stupid of me! Why did I say yes? Who knows whether a cat waits somewhere!"

But all the way long,
followed anxiously by the
little mouse, the red shoe
hopped and sang songs.

They walked a long way.

A big black cat lay on a porch, basking in the sun.

DA DA DA DA !
DA DA DA DA ! DA DA DA DA ! DA DA DA !

"Who is singing?" But before he could figure out where the singing came from, he saw the little mouse walking toward him.

"I can't believe it!" growled the cat. "A little mouse parading before me? How outrageous!" Beside himself, he dashed like lightning to the little mouse.

MeOw

Up jumped the shoe and slapped the cat. The black cat gave a painful wail and fell back onto the porch.

"Oh no! What happened? The stars are falling like raindrops!" the cat meowed.

Hearing the noise, a girl appeared. "What happened, kitty?" As she cuddled the cat, she noticed the red shoe. "Red shoe! Red shoe!" she shouted with joy. "It's my poor lonely lost red shoe!" Cradling the cat in one arm, she picked up the red shoe and went back inside. The little mouse took his chance and climbed into the trash can.

Two red shoes now lay side by side on the shoe rack, talking softly to each other.

I MISSED YOU A LOT!

I MISSED YOU, TOO!

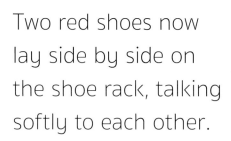

"A little mouse helped me find you!"
"We should really thank the little mouse."
"Yes, we should..."

The little mouse
hid in the trash can
and listened. Their
soft voices sounded
incredibly beautiful.

At midnight, the trash was taken
outside the city.
The little mouse crawled out and, in
the silver moonlight, slowly walked to
his little house at the forest's edge.

The emptiness in his heart was, indeed, different from being hungry. For the first time, he realized the road home alone was so quiet. "How wonderful it would be if a mouse were waiting for me in my house!" he thought.

STARFISH BAY
CHILDREN'S BOOKS

An Imprint of Starfish Bay Publishing
www.starfishbaypublishing.com
STARFISH BAY is a trademark of Starfish Bay Publishing Pty Ltd.

ALL SHOES COME IN TWOS

This edition © Starfish Bay Publishing, 2018
Printed and bound in China by Beijing Shangtang Print & Packaging Co., Ltd.
11 Tengren Road, Niulanshan Town, Shunyi District, Beijing, China
ISBN 978 1 76036 037 5

Sincere thanks to Courtney Chow, Jenny Crowhurst, Marlo Garnsworthy, Dan Hu, Belinda Piscino and Elyse Williams (in alphabetical order) from Starfish Bay Children's Books for editing and/or translating this book.

Starfish Bay Children's Books would also like to thank Elyse Williams for her creative efforts in preparing this edition for publication.

Other titles by the same author, Sulan TANG